0

A NOTE TO PARENTS

When your children are ready to "step into reading," giving them the right books is as crucial as giving them the right food to eat. **Step into Reading Books** present exciting stories and information reinforced with lively, colorful illustrations that make learning to read fun, satisfying, and worthwhile. They are priced so that acquiring an entire library of them is affordable. And they are beginning readers with a difference—they're written on five levels.

Early Step into Reading Books are designed for brand-new readers, with large type and only one or two lines of very simple text per page. **Step 1 Books** feature the same easy-to-read type as the Early Step into Reading Books, but with more words per page. **Step 2 Books** are both longer and slightly more difficult, while **Step 3 Books** introduce readers to paragraphs and fully developed plot lines. **Step 4 Books** offer exciting nonfiction for the increasingly independent reader.

The grade levels assigned to the five steps—preschool through kindergarten for the Early Books, preschool through grade 1 for Step 1, grades 1 through 3 for Step 2, grades 2 through 3 for Step 3, and grades 2 through 4 for Step 4—are intended only as guides. Some children move through all five steps very rapidly; others climb the steps over a period of several years. Either way, these books will help your child "step into reading" in style!

As always, with much love to my family. And again,
with much affection and appreciation to Heidi.
—L.G.

To my sisters, Tamar and Trummy, treasures in my life.
—B.S.T.

Text copyright © 2000 by Lois Grambling. Illustrations copyright © 2000 by Bridget Starr Taylor.
All rights reserved under International and Pan-American Copyright Conventions. Published in
the United States by Random House, Inc., New York, and simultaneously in Canada by Random
House of Canada Limited, Toronto.

www.randomhouse.com/kids

Library of Congress Cataloging-in-Publication Data
Grambling, Lois G.
Miss Hildy's missing cape caper / by Lois Grambling ; illustrated by Bridget Starr Taylor.
p. cm. — (Step into reading. A step 2 book)
SUMMARY: Miss Hildy must use her detective skills again when she discovers that her
detecting cap and cape are missing.
ISBN 0-375-80196-0 (pbk.) — ISBN 0-375-90196-5 (lib. bdg.)
[1. Halloween—Fiction. 2. Flamingos—Fiction. 3. Mystery and detective stories.]
I. Taylor, Bridget Starr, 1959– ill. II. Title. III. Series: Step into reading. Step 2 book.
PZ7.G7655Mi 2000 [Fic]—dc21 99-13129
Printed in the United States of America July 2000 10 9 8 7 6 5 4 3 2 1

STEP INTO READING, RANDOM HOUSE, and the Random House colophon are registered
trademarks and the Step into Reading colophon is a trademark of Random House, Inc.

Step into Reading®

Miss Hildy's
Missing Cape Caper

by Lois Grambling

illustrated by Bridget Starr Taylor

A Step 2 Book

Random House 🏠 New York

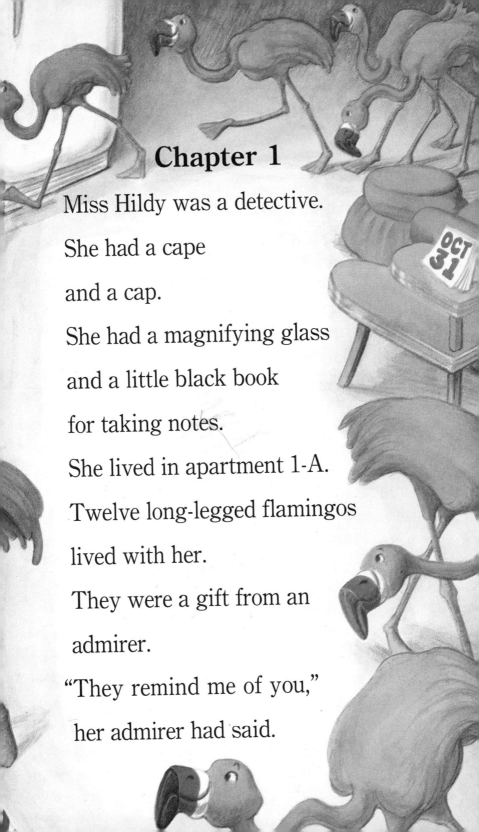

Chapter 1

Miss Hildy was a detective.

She had a cape

and a cap.

She had a magnifying glass

and a little black book

for taking notes.

She lived in apartment 1-A.

Twelve long-legged flamingos

lived with her.

They were a gift from an

admirer.

"They remind me of you,"

her admirer had said.

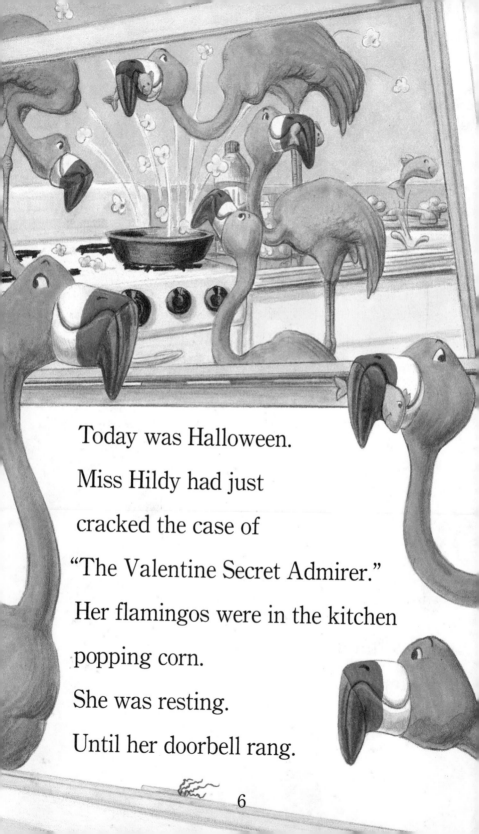

Today was Halloween.

Miss Hildy had just

cracked the case of

"The Valentine Secret Admirer."

Her flamingos were in the kitchen

popping corn.

She was resting.

Until her doorbell rang.

Miss Hildy opened the door.

But no one was there.

"Probably a Halloween prankster,"

she said.

Miss Hildy closed the door.

Her detective eye spotted something.

The coat rack was empty!

Her cape and cap were missing!

Miss Hildy smelled a mystery.

Or maybe it was the fish

her flamingos had for supper.

Either way, Miss Hildy

had a mystery to solve.

Who stole her detective cape

and cap?

Chapter 2

Miss Hildy could hardly wait
to start detecting.
But what would she wear?
She had no detective cape or
cap now!
Then she remembered a
witch costume that she had
in her closet.
It had a cape.
She dug it out
and put it on.

But something else was missing.

Her magnifying glass!

Her little black book!

They were in her cape pockets.

How could she look for clues?

Or take notes?

Then she remembered
the spyglass her flamingos used
for bird watching.
She remembered the grocery list
she had started that morning.
She would have to use those.
Miss Hildy was back in business!

Chapter 3

Miss Hildy started looking

for clues.

She checked the coat rack.

Her detective eye found nothing.

She checked the window.

Her detective eye saw that

it was open.

Some red threads were stuck
on the windowsill.
"Aha!" she said. "Two clues."
She wrote down:
open window
red threads

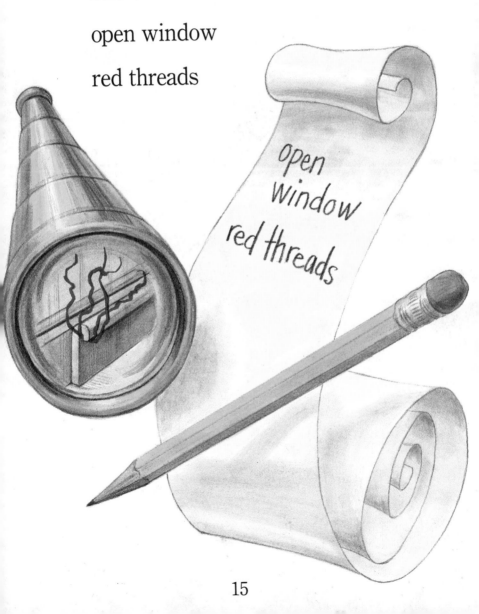

Miss Hildy leaned out the window.

She checked the ground below.

Her detective eye spotted something.

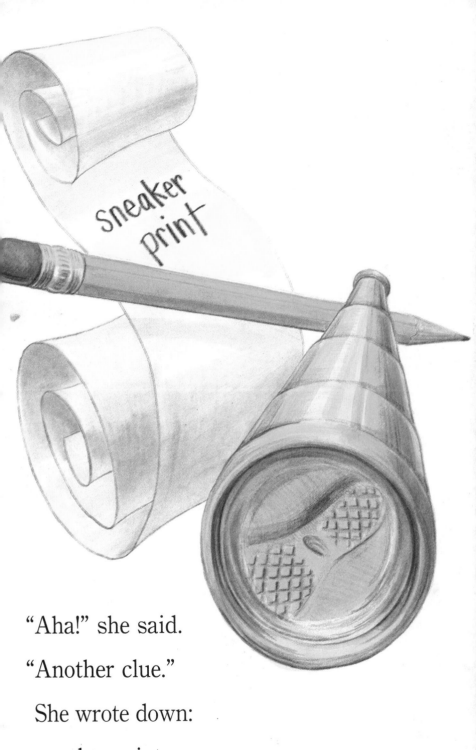

"Aha!" she said.

"Another clue."

She wrote down:

sneaker print

Miss Hildy's detective eye
found no more clues.
"Time to review,"
Miss Hildy said.

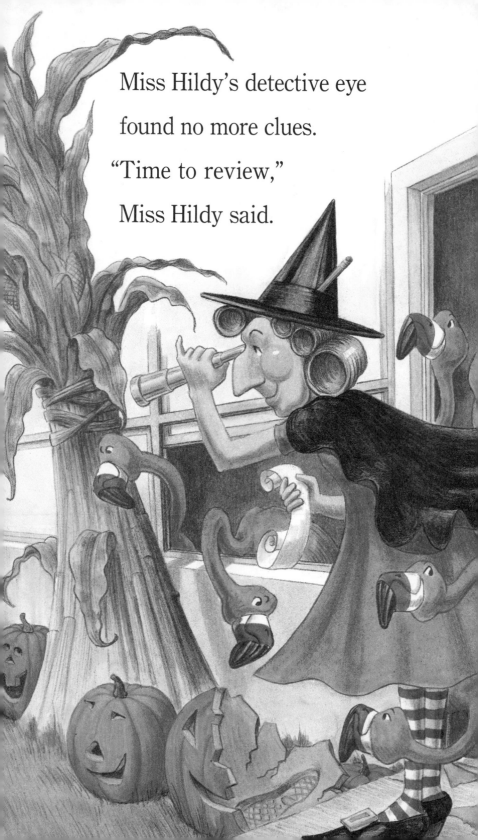

She read the clues out loud:
"Peanut butter,

jelly,

bread.

Oops! Wrong side!"

Miss Hildy turned the list over

and read:

"Open window,

red threads,

sneaker print."

"Hmmm," Miss Hildy said.

"The thief is tall.

Tall enough to reach into

my open window.

Tall enough to grab my cape and cap

off the coat rack.

And…the thief is probably

wearing sneakers!"

Miss Hildy was ready
to go out looking for the thief.
But before she did,
she asked her flamingos
to pop enough corn
for the trick-or-treaters.
AND DID THEY EVER!

Chapter 4

Miss Hildy scanned the street.

She saw some trick-or-treaters.

One was wearing a cape.

"A suspect!" she said.

The suspect ran onto a porch.

"He could be the thief!"

Miss Hildy took out her grocery list.

She wrote down:

Dracula

Miss Hildy looked through the spyglass.

"But no, his cape is black," she said.

"Besides, he is too short."

Miss Hildy crossed off Dracula.

Miss Hildy saw some more
trick-or-treaters.

"Another cape," she said.

And this one was *red!*

"She could be the thief!"

Miss Hildy wrote down:

Red Riding Hood

Miss Hildy looked closer.

"But no, her cape has a hood,"
she said.

"Besides, she is too short."

Miss Hildy crossed off
Red Riding Hood.

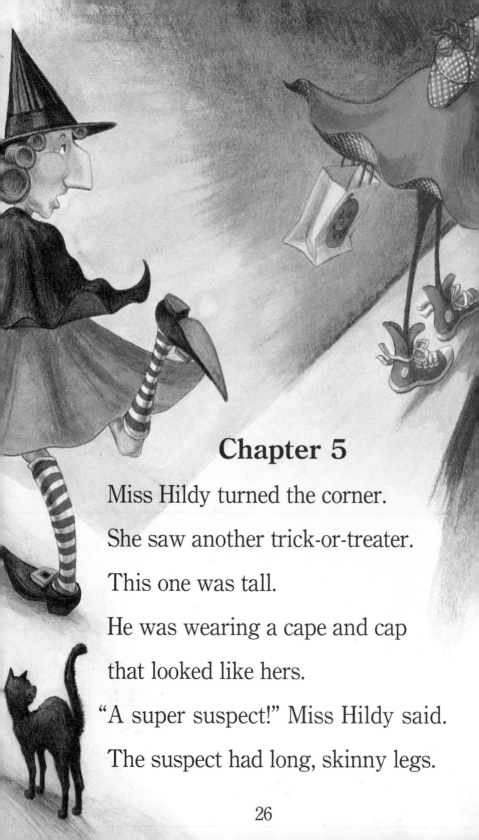

Chapter 5

Miss Hildy turned the corner.

She saw another trick-or-treater.

This one was tall.

He was wearing a cape and cap

that looked like hers.

"A super suspect!" Miss Hildy said.

The suspect had long, skinny legs.

"That must be Leggy Lewis,"
Miss Hildy said.
"He lives in apartment 1-B.
He could be the thief!"
She wrote down:
Leggy Lewis

When Miss Hildy looked up,

her super suspect was gone.

"Drat," she said.

"He slipped away.

Oh, my poor pinched toes.
I will go home and
wait for Leggy there."

Chapter 6

Miss Hildy was back home.
She kicked off
the pointy witch shoes.
"Ahhh, that's better!" she said.
"Now I know why witches
ride on broomsticks."

A ghost came down the walk.

It headed toward apartment 1-B.

The ghost was tall.

It was wearing a short sheet.

Miss Hildy's detective eye
spotted long, skinny legs.
Like Leggy Lewis's.

"Is that you, Leggy?"

Miss Hildy called.

"It's me all right," said Leggy.

Miss Hildy slipped into

her slippers.

She limped over to Leggy.

"Were you a ghost all night?"

she asked him.

"Sure was," Leggy said.

"Drat!" said Miss Hildy.

She crossed Leggy Lewis off her list.

Miss Hildy began to worry.

She had no more suspects.

Unless…

Miss Hildy had a thought.

Chapter 7

"Leggy," Miss Hildy asked,

"did you see a tall trick-or-treater

tonight?"

Leggy nodded.

"Was he wearing a detective cape

and cap?"

Leggy took off his sheet.

"Yes," he said.

"And whoever it was,

it sure did

remind me of you."

Miss Hildy gasped.

Those words!

She had heard them before!

"Of course!" she said.

"Now it's as clear

as the nose on my face!"

"Let me get one thing straight,"
Miss Hildy said.

"You saw a trick-or-treater

that *reminded you of me?*"

"That is correct," said Leggy.

He handed Miss Hildy a treat.

Miss Hildy wrote CASE CLOSED
across her grocery list.
"Thank you for helping me
crack this case, Leggy,"
she said.
"And thank you for the popcorn."

Chapter 8

Miss Hildy went
into her apartment.
Her detective eye spotted
her cape and cap!

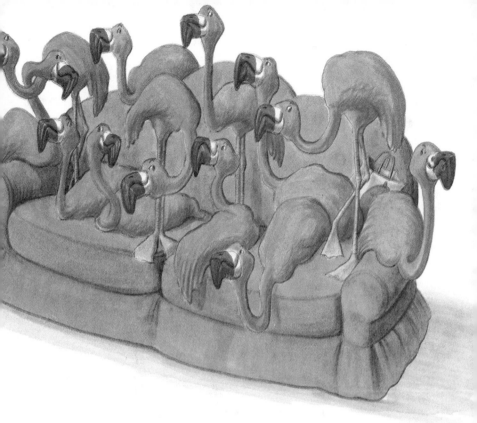

Her twelve flamingos were
sitting on the sofa.
"So, which one of you
went out tonight
in my detective cape and cap?"
she asked.
Not one flamingo
fluttered a feather.

Miss Hildy put on her detective cape and cap.

She took out her magnifying glass.

She checked her flamingos for clues.

Her detective eye found nothing…

until she came to Number Twelve.

Her detective eye found

chocolate on his beak.

Her detective nose smelled

peppermint on his breath.

"Aha!" she said. "*You* are the one!"

Number Twelve reached

behind his back.

He pulled out a bag full of treats.

"For me?" she asked.

Number Twelve nodded.

"How sweet," Miss Hildy said.

She nibbled a chocolate truffle.

"Please—help yourselves,"

said Miss Hildy to the flamingos.

AND DID THEY EVER!

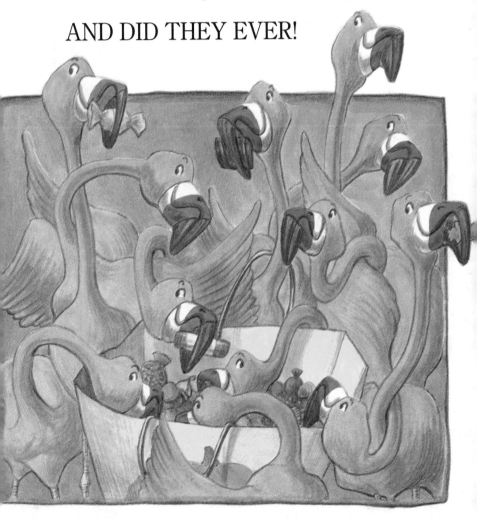

Miss Hildy had an idea.
She grabbed a bolt of red cloth
from her closet floor.
"I will make each of you
a cape and cap like mine,"
she said.

"Then you will look like me.
And next Halloween we can
go trick-or-treating together."

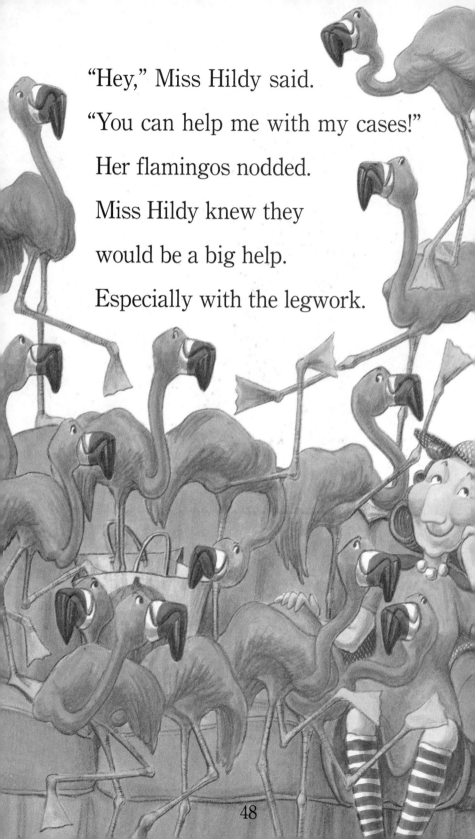

"Hey," Miss Hildy said.

"You can help me with my cases!"

Her flamingos nodded.

Miss Hildy knew they

would be a big help.

Especially with the legwork.